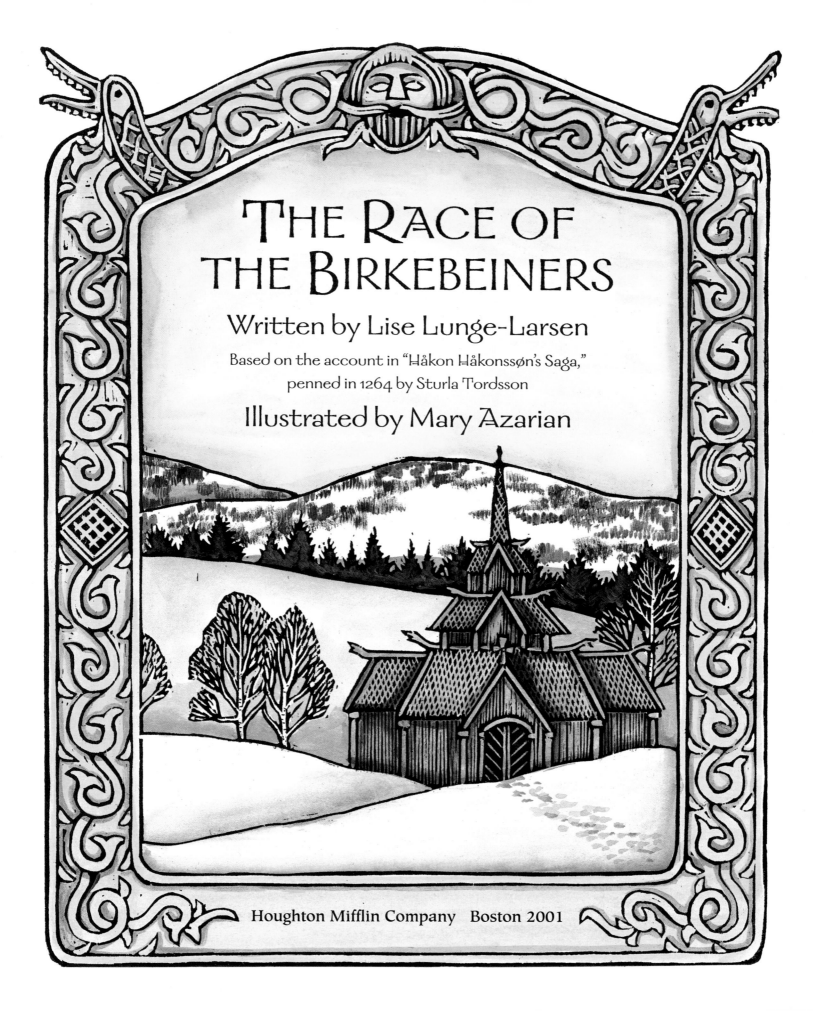

THE RACE OF
THE BIRKEBEINERS

Written by Lise Lunge-Larsen

Based on the account in "Håkon Håkonssøn's Saga,"
penned in 1264 by Sturla Tordsson

Illustrated by Mary Azarian

Houghton Mifflin Company   Boston 2001

THE BIRKEBEINERS were the fiercest and bravest warriors that ever lived in Norway. They could fight on land as well as at sea. They could hide for weeks on end in the woods without getting caught. And they could sleep through snowstorms by burying themselves in drifts and putting their shields on top for protection.

The Birkebeiners were the king's loyal men. They despised the Baglers, those rich nobles and false bishops who wanted to line their pockets with the peasants' money. The Birkebeiners, you see, were mostly peasants. When they went into battle they wore no costly armor, just birchbark wrapped around their legs, and so they were called "Birkebeiners," which means "Birchleggers."

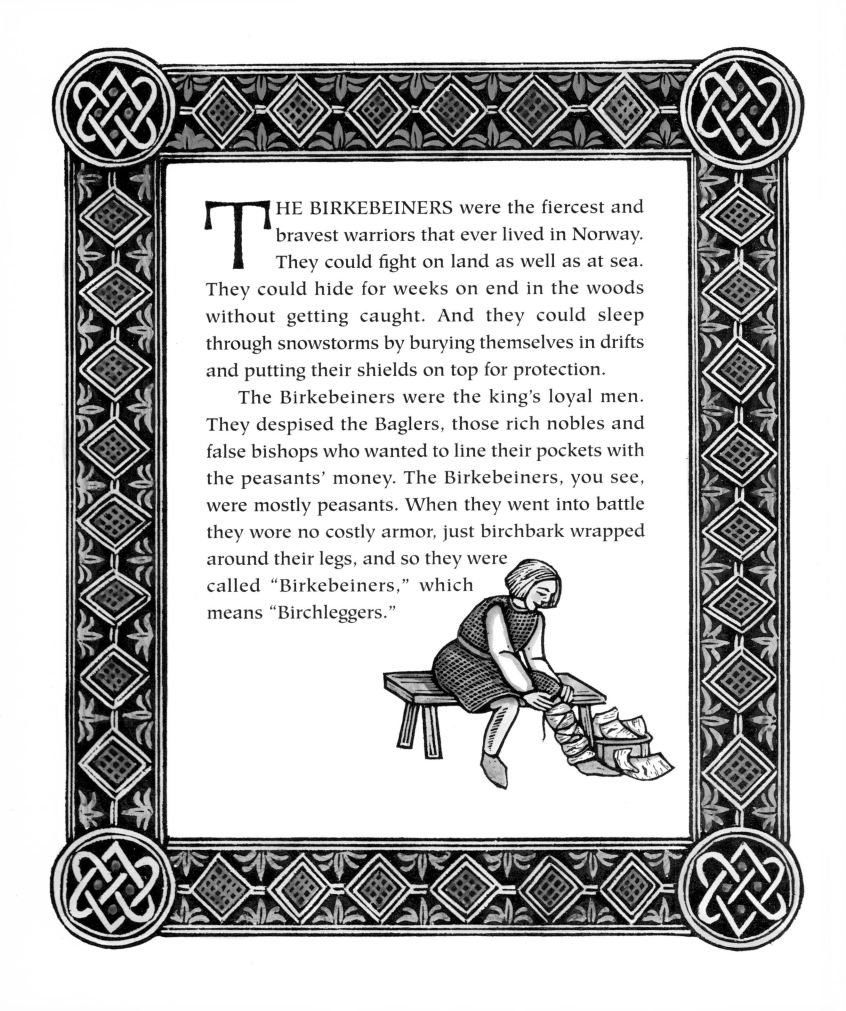

THIS STORY BEGINS on Christmas Eve in the year 1206, at a small wooden farm belonging to the district governor, a proud Birkebeiner. All the folk at the farm had gathered to celebrate Holy Night, and the little house glowed with the light of dozens of candles. A bright fire burned in the center of the room and a thick layer of straw covered the floor. Tonight, everyone from the littlest herd boy to the master and mistress of the house would sleep together in the straw, in memory of the Christ child born in a stable so long ago.

THE GOVERNOR had just lifted his drinking horn in a toast when there was a knock at the door. Quickly, the men reached for their swords. Ever since the death of the king a year and a half ago, the Baglers had been raiding Birkebeiner farms. But surely they wouldn't come to kill them on Christmas Eve?

GRABBING HIS BATTLE-AX, the governor went to the door and bellowed, "Who comes?"

"It's Sira Trond," came the answer.

"Sira Trond! Come in. You frightened us."

The priest stepped in and shook the snow from his cloak.

"What brings you so far from home on Christmas Eve?" asked the governor. Sira Trond reached out a hand, and a young woman carrying a baby stepped inside.

"This is Inga of Varteig and Prince Håkon (HO-kun)," he said.

NOW THE BIRKEBEINERS had all heard that a prince was born three weeks after the death of the king, but they had never expected to see the baby alive. Surely the Baglers, who wanted a king of their own on the throne, had killed him. And, yet, here he was.

"I have hidden them for over a year," explained Sira Trond. "But now the Baglers have become so strong in the south and their raids so frequent, we had to escape, and so we came here."

"YOU ARE WELCOME," said the governor. "Stay as long as you like."

But even the home of the governor was not safe for long. Almost overnight the Baglers had learned of their escape and were coming after them on horses. There was no time to lose. They had to flee north, to Nidaros, where the many Birkebeiner chieftains could protect them.

TO OUTWIT THE BAGLERS, they would ski across the mountains to the east and head north to Nidaros from there. The Baglers would never imagine them crossing these mountains, for they were some of the tallest and stormiest in all of Norway. The small group would be leaving at the darkest and coldest time of the year. And they would travel when hosts of evil spirits roamed the land looking for unprotected humans to snatch up. But there was no other way. They had to cross those mountains if they were to save Prince Håkon from the Baglers.

Sira Trond, Inga, and Håkon went immediately to a small town called Lillehammer. There eight Birkebeiners joined them, including Torstein Skevla (TOR-stine SHEV-la) and Skervald Skrukka (SHER-vol SKRU-ka), two of the best skiers in all of Norway. Torstein was big and broad, with immense arms and legs. A red beard covered his face. Skervald was fair and clean-shaven, with playful eyes. Tall and slender, he almost flew on top of the snow and easily kept up with Torstein's powerful skiing. For years they had raced each other for fun. Now they would race to defeat the Baglers.

AFTER A HASTY MEAL of dried mutton, flatbread, barley porridge, and strong ale, everyone was ready to ski. Although they hoped to avoid battle, they wrapped birchbark on top of their breeches, pulled iron helmets over their skin caps, and fetched spears, axes, and shields.

INGA MADE HERSELF READY, too. She put on a beautiful wool cloak over her long dress and pinned on a magnificent gold brooch. It was a gift from King Håkon before he died. Baby Håkon would nestle down in a sheepskin bag with the wool on the inside. Inga would carry him on her back.

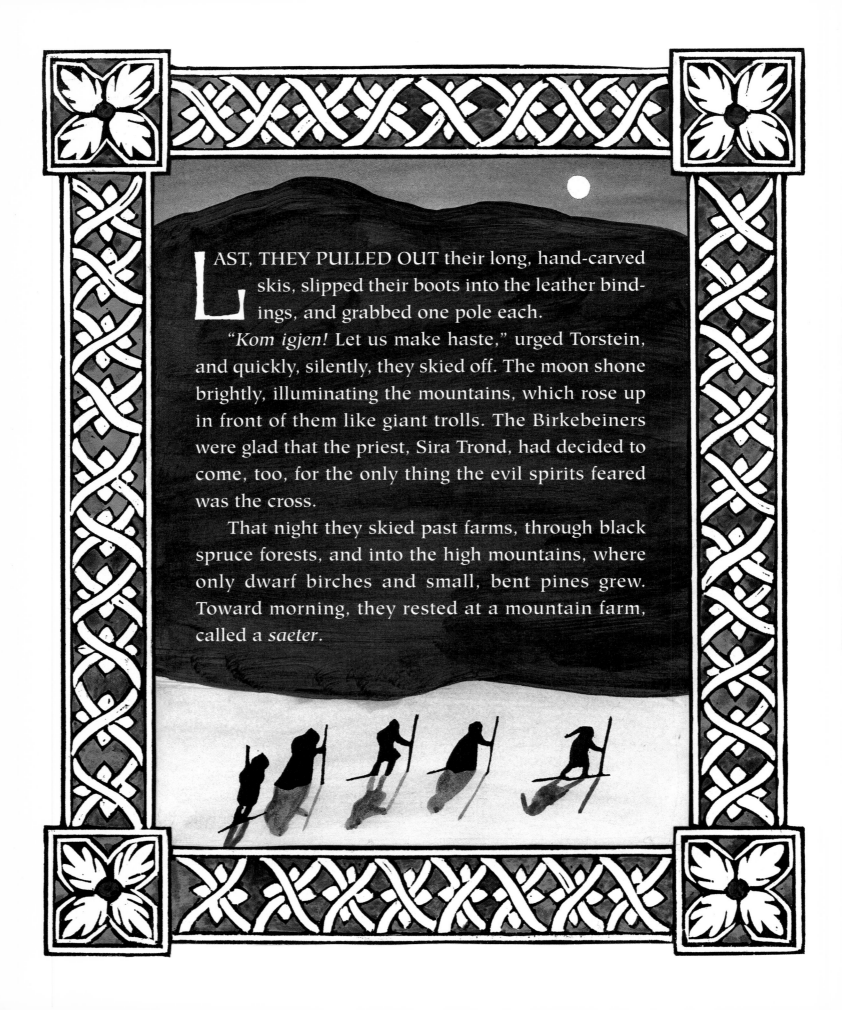

L AST, THEY PULLED OUT their long, hand-carved skis, slipped their boots into the leather bind-ings, and grabbed one pole each.

"*Kom igjen!* Let us make haste," urged Torstein, and quickly, silently, they skied off. The moon shone brightly, illuminating the mountains, which rose up in front of them like giant trolls. The Birkebeiners were glad that the priest, Sira Trond, had decided to come, too, for the only thing the evil spirits feared was the cross.

That night they skied past farms, through black spruce forests, and into the high mountains, where only dwarf birches and small, bent pines grew. Toward morning, they rested at a mountain farm, called a *saeter*.

A BITING WIND gusted up when they set out again. Soon heavy snow began to fall. The farther they skied into the mountains, the faster and fiercer the snow fell. It blinded their eyes and stung their cheeks, but they hunched their shoulders and skied on.

ALL DAY they struggled. When darkness fell, the storm only strengthened. They were high above the tree line, where nothing blocked the force of the wind and the snow. They could barely see the tips of their own skis.

AT LAST their guide stopped. "I don't know where we are," he said. "We shall have to dig a shelter in the snow and wait out the storm."

"This storm could last for days," said Torstein. "Håkon will never survive. Let me take him and ski ahead. I can ski faster alone, and the baby must be brought to a warm shelter soon."

"I will go with you," said Skervald.

Inga regarded the two men. Then she looked down at Prince Håkon. Since his birth, the two of them had never been apart. If she gave him up now, she might never see him again.

Quickly, she loosened a silver cross from around her neck and stuffed it into Håkon's sheepskin bag for protection. Then she handed her baby to Torstein. It was her only chance to save her son's life.

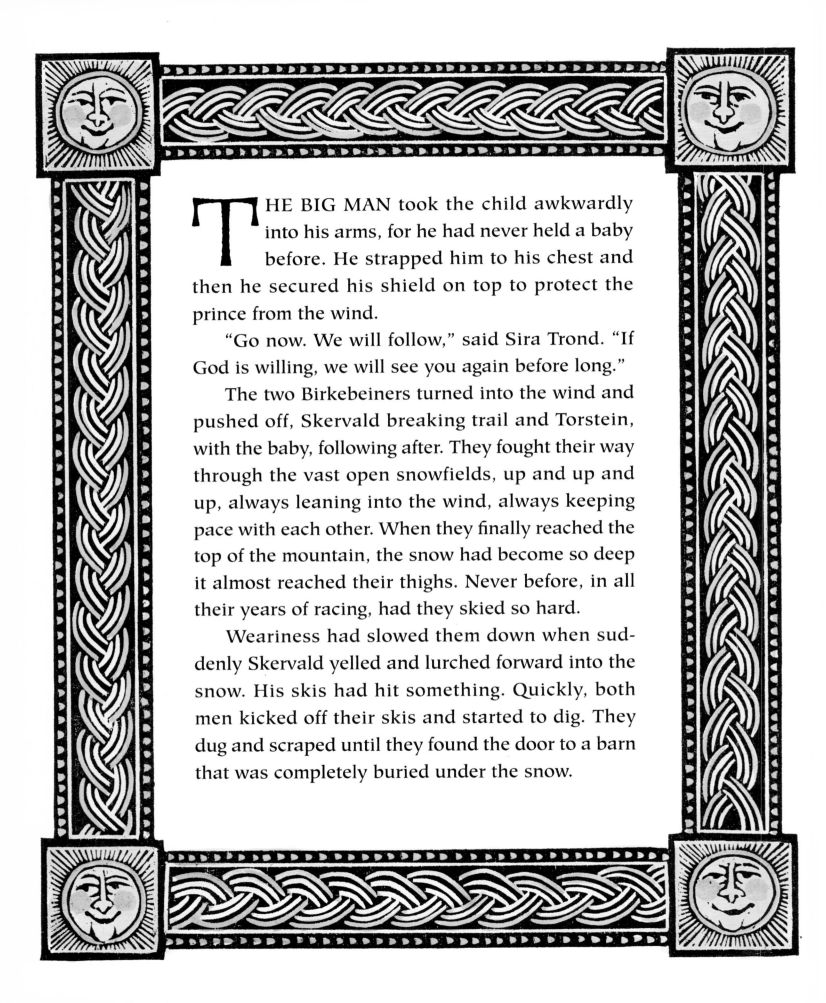

T HE BIG MAN took the child awkwardly into his arms, for he had never held a baby before. He strapped him to his chest and then he secured his shield on top to protect the prince from the wind.

"Go now. We will follow," said Sira Trond. "If God is willing, we will see you again before long."

The two Birkebeiners turned into the wind and pushed off, Skervald breaking trail and Torstein, with the baby, following after. They fought their way through the vast open snowfields, up and up and up, always leaning into the wind, always keeping pace with each other. When they finally reached the top of the mountain, the snow had become so deep it almost reached their thighs. Never before, in all their years of racing, had they skied so hard.

Weariness had slowed them down when suddenly Skervald yelled and lurched forward into the snow. His skis had hit something. Quickly, both men kicked off their skis and started to dig. They dug and scraped until they found the door to a barn that was completely buried under the snow.

ONCE INSIDE, Skervald made a fire with his flint and steel. Torstein lifted Håkon out of his fur. He was so cold and white that at first Torstein thought he had died! But then the baby started to move and to whimper a little. Skervald looked up from the fire.

"Look, he is hungry," he said, pointing to Håkon, who was sucking his thumb as hard as he could.

"All we have is snow," said Torstein. So Skervald fetched snow and fed the baby lump after tiny lump to melt in his mouth.

Soon a fire was burning and the two men curled up to sleep, Håkon snug in Torstein's arms. In the middle of the night, there was a loud noise outside and the door burst open. In came the rest of the Birkebeiners with Inga at the head. They had found the barn!

AFTER THREE LONG DAYS, the storm died down. The skiers had had nothing but snow to eat, but they skied on, down the mountain, and that night they reached the valley below. Here they rested before traveling to Nidaros, where the Birkebeiner chieftains welcomed them.

NOW, IF THIS WERE A FAIRY TALE, the story would be over. But this story is true, and what happened next is perhaps most miraculous of all.

The Baglers would not give up looking for ways to get rid of Prince Håkon. They started a rumor throughout Norway that he was not the true son of the king and demanded that Inga undergo the Ordeal of the Burning Irons.

For months the rumors spread and grew. Finally, to prove that her son was indeed the true prince, Inga agreed to the test. And now there was nothing the Birkebeiners could do to save their little prince, except watch.

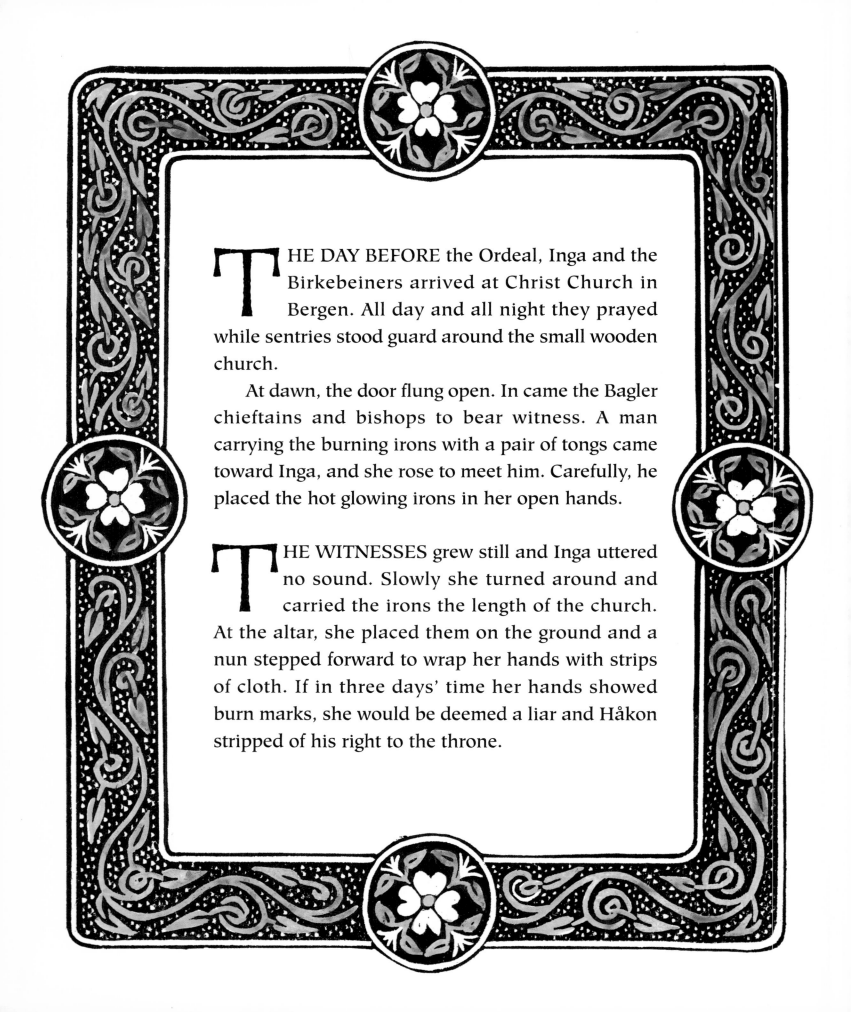

THE DAY BEFORE the Ordeal, Inga and the Birkebeiners arrived at Christ Church in Bergen. All day and all night they prayed while sentries stood guard around the small wooden church.

At dawn, the door flung open. In came the Bagler chieftains and bishops to bear witness. A man carrying the burning irons with a pair of tongs came toward Inga, and she rose to meet him. Carefully, he placed the hot glowing irons in her open hands.

THE WITNESSES grew still and Inga uttered no sound. Slowly she turned around and carried the irons the length of the church. At the altar, she placed them on the ground and a nun stepped forward to wrap her hands with strips of cloth. If in three days' time her hands showed burn marks, she would be deemed a liar and Håkon stripped of his right to the throne.

To Steve, my own Birkebeiner, and to all the Ingas
who keep me company on the trails
—L. L.-L.

To the memory of Jackrabbit Johansen, intrepid cross-country skier
from Québec, who at age ninety still skied twenty miles a day
—M. A.

Author's Note

MOST OF WHAT WE KNOW about Prince Håkon we learn from "Håkon Håkonssøn's Saga," which records the entire life story of Prince Håkon. Essentially, all events in my story are true. The saga's account of Håkon's escape is brief, for, like most saga writers, Sturla Tordsson was more interested in recording events than in describing the landscape, people's feelings, customs, or beliefs. For example, the saga tells us that Inga and Sira Trond arrived at the district governor's house on Christmas Eve, but it says nothing about how this holy night was celebrated. Other sources helped me flesh out that scene. Furthermore, the saga tells us nothing about how Inga might have felt when she handed over her child to Torstein and Skervald, nor does it tell us which one of them carried the prince. However, the saga does record that the men had nothing but snow to feed the baby.

Selected Bibliography

Alnæs, Karsten. *The History of Norway: There Lies a Land.* Oslo: Gyldendal, 1996.
Bø, Olav. *Our Norwegian Christmas.* Oslo: Det Norske Samlaget, 1974.
———. *Skiing Through History.* Oslo: Det Norske Samlaget, 1992.
Brendalsmo, Jan, et al. *Life in the Middle Ages.* Oslo: Mykle Illustrasjoner, 1996.
Emblem, Terje, et al. *Norway I: Norway's History Before 1850.* Oslo: J. W. Cappelens Forlag, 1997.
Tordsson, Sturla. "Håkon Håkonssøn's Saga" in *Norway's Kings' Sagas in Four Volumes.* Ill. by Gerhard Munthe. Kristiania:
    J. M. Stenersen Forlag, 1913–1914.
Vaage, Jacob. *The World of Skiing.* Oslo: Hjemmenes Forlag, 1979.

Text copyright © 2001 by Lise Lunge-Larsen
Illustrations copyright © 2001 by Mary Azarian

www.houghtonmifflinbooks.com

The text of this book is set in 14-point Hiroshige.
The illustrations are woodcuts, hand-tinted with watercolors.

Library of Congress Cataloging-in-Publication Data

Lunge-Larsen, Lise.
The race of the Birkenbeiners / written by Lise Lunge-Larsen ; illustrated by Mary Azarian. p. cm.
Summary: Tells how the infant Prince Håkon is rescued by men fiercely loyal to his dead father,
who ski across the rugged mountains in blizzard conditions to save him from his enemies, the Baglers.
ISBN 0-618-10313-9
1. Håkon IV Håkonssøn, King of Norway, 1204–1263—Legends. [1. Håkon IV Håkonssøn,
King of Norway, 1204–1263—Legends. 2. Folklore—Norway.] I. Azarian, Mary, ill. II. Title.
PZ8.1.L9735 Rac 2001   398.2'09481'02—dc21   00-053977

Manufactured in the United States of America
BVG 10 9 8 7 6 5 4 3 2 1